SUPER CUTE SKETCHBOOK

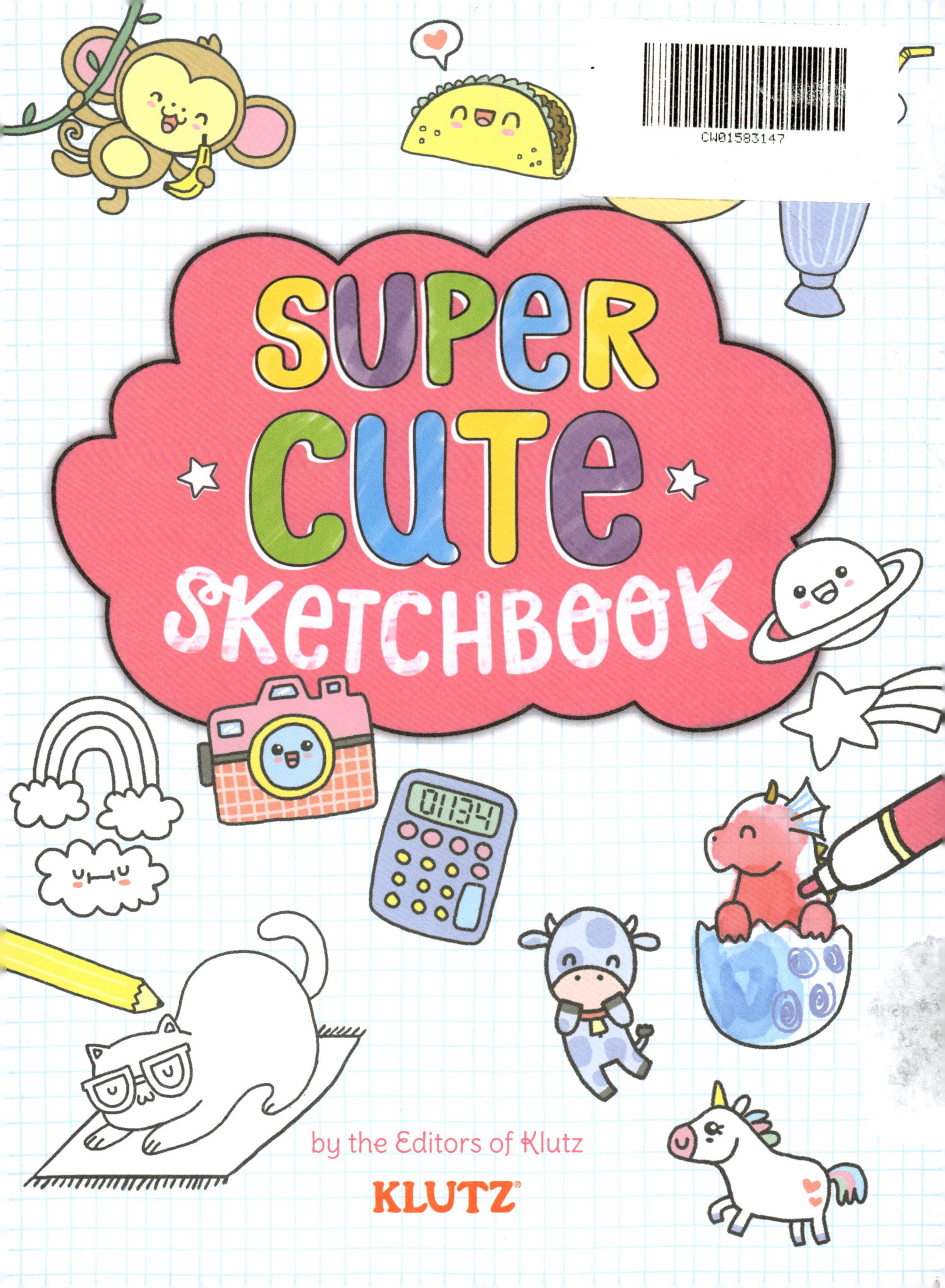

by the Editors of Klutz

KLUTZ

KLUTZ® creates activity [illegible]s and other great stuff for kids ages 3 to 103. We began our corporate life [illegible]n a garage we shared with a Chevrolet Impala. Although we've outgrown that first office, Klutz g[illegible]c headquarters is still staffed entirely by real human beings. For those of you who collect mission statements, here's ours:

CREATE WONDERFUL THINGS • BE YOURSELF • HAVE FUN!

Markers made in Wenzhou, China. Book printed in Jiaxing, China. 68

WRITE US

We would love to hear your comments regarding this or any of our books.

KLUTZ®
557 Broadway
New York, NY 10012
thefolks@klutz.com

For information regarding permission, please contact Klutz, Attn: Permissions Department, 557 Broadway, New York, NY 10012.

For UK or EU safety or quality concerns, please contact (UK) **www.scholastic.co.uk/productinformation** or (EU) **www.scholastic.ie/productinformation**

Distributed in the UK by
Scholastic UK Ltd
Bosworth Avenue
Warwick, CV34 6UQ
United Kingdom

Distributed in Australia by
Scholastic Australia Ltd
PO Box 579
Gosford, NSW
Australia 2250

Distributed in Hong Kong by
Scholastic Hong Kong Ltd
Suites 2001-2, Top Glory Tower
262 Gloucester Road
Causeway Bay, Hong Kong

Distributed in the EU by
Scholastic Ltd
Unit 89E, Lagan Road
Dublin Industrial Estate
Glasnevin, Dublin 11 HP5F
Ireland

Distributed in Canada by
Scholastic Canada Ltd
604 King Street West
Toronto, Ontario
Canada M5V 1E1

ISBN 979-8-225-03260-9
4 1 5 8 5 7 0 8 8 8

FSC® www.fsc.org MIX Paper | Supporting responsible forestry FSC® C135401

We make Klutz books using resources that have been approved according to the FSC® standard, which is managed by the Forest Stewardship Council®. This means the paper in this book comes from well managed FSC®-certified forests and other controlled sources.

TABLE OF CONTENTS

WHAT YOU GET

DOUBLE-TIPPED MARKERS

You get 8 different colors with these 4 super sweet markers.

You can use black ink to add outlines and details to your adorable doodles.

OTHER STUFF YOU'LL NEED

Pencil

Eraser

Other markers and colored pencils

Tracing paper

Other drawing paper

TIPS FOR USING YOUR MARKERS

The paper in this book is designed to be used with your markers. If you want to use your own paper, test a marker on a corner to check if the ink bleeds through. That means the paper is too thin.

Don't draw on yourself. If you accidentally get ink on your skin, wash it off with warm, soapy water.

When you're done crafting, store your markers in the plastic case on the cover. Keep your supplies away from babies and pets.

When you're not coloring with your markers, cap them tightly to make the ink last longer.

HOW TO COLOR WITH YOUR MARKERS

Use the tip of your marker to make thin lines.

Use the wide side of your marker to make thick lines.

Overlapping marker lines will create a darker color.

To mix colors, color with the lighter color first and let it dry. Then color over it with the second (darker) marker.

REMARKABLE!

Use this page to test out your new super sweet markers and try the coloring techniques in the spaces and designs below.

The thin tip of your marker will make it easier to color in the watermelon's rind.

Make the outside of the peel darker by overlapping yellow strokes.

Try using the side of your marker to color in the apple.

Layer strokes of the blue marker to get a darker blue color.

HOW TO DRAW CUTE STUFF

With a little practice, you can draw anything adorable in four easy steps.

WHAT YOU'LL NEED:

Pencil

Eraser

Super sweet markers

1. SKETCH: With a pencil, lightly draw the outlines of your doodle. Don't worry if it isn't perfect—just keep sketching until you get the shape that you want.

2. ADD COLOR: Use your markers to color in your darling doodle!

3. INK: Trace over the outlines with your black marker.

4. ERASE: Once all the ink is dry, erase the pencil marks from Step 1.

SKETCH A VEGGIE

Practice sketching, coloring, inking, and erasing with the veggies below.

FRUITY CUTIES

Strawberry

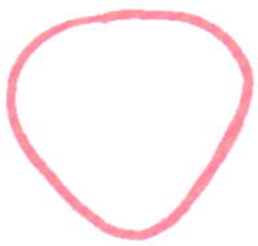

1 Sketch a triangle with rounded corners.

2 Draw two leaves at the top.

3 Add a face.

4 Draw seeds all over the fruit.

5 Color in your sweet strawberry!

Watermelon

1 Sketch a half circle.

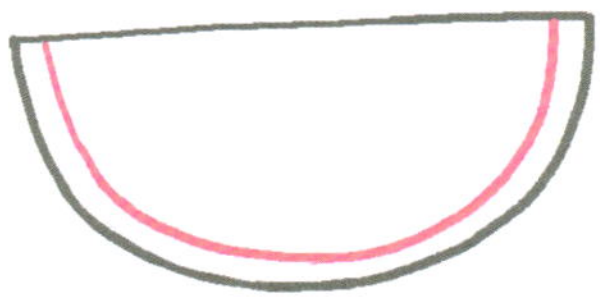

2 Make a line around the curve for the rind.

3 Add a face.

4 Draw in seeds.

5 Add color to complete this cutie!

Pack a Picnic

Add some sweet fruits to this yummy picnic lunch.
Draw some fruity flavor in the lemonade, too.

EXPRESS YOURSELF

Your doodles don't have to be all smiles all the time. Here are some mini moods that you can draw.

TIP

For maximum cuteness, make the mouth line up with the eyes.

DUMPLING SOUP

The dumplings in this bowl of noodle soup look a bit blank. Draw in some faces to make them happy, sad, sleepy, or make up any kind of mood you want.

SWEET TREATS

Ice-Cream Cone

1 Draw a circle.

2 Erase the bottom, and sketch a little ruffle.

3 Add a face.

4 Draw in a cone at the bottom.

5 Add crosshatches and color to finish.

TIP
For a crisp outline, color the pencil sketch first. Then draw the outline on top with your black marker.

Donut

1 Draw a circle.

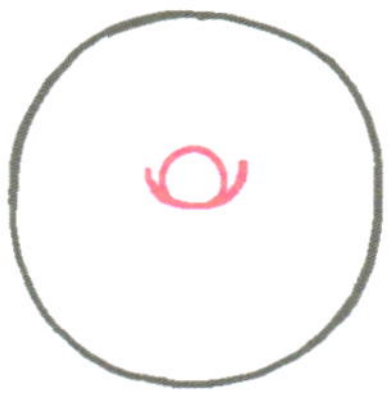

2 Make two curved lines for the hole.

3 Add a face.

4 Draw a wavy circle for the frosting.

5 Add sprinkles and color in your donut.

Dessert Dreams

Are you craving a sweet treat? Sketch it out! Fill in this box of donuts and draw ice-cream scoops into the cones.

TIME TO EAT

Toaster

1 Draw a half circle with a small line at the top.

2 Add handles and legs.

3 Sketch in a slice of bread.

4 Add faces.

5 Draw a plug and add color. Ink the outlines and erase your pencil marks.

Fried Egg & Waffle

1 Draw a circle for the yolk.

2 Add a face.

3 Draw a puddle shape around the yolk for the egg white.

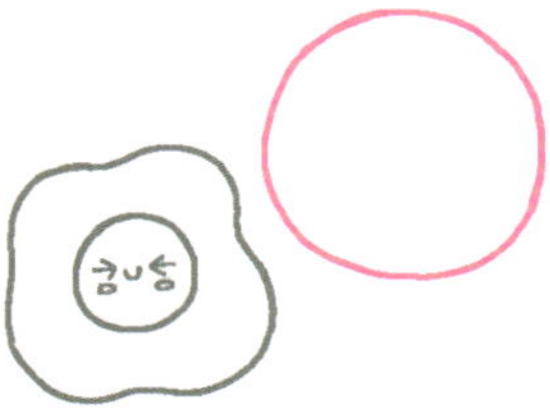

4 Draw a circle for the waffle.

5 Add a face.

6 Add grid lines and color.

Burger

1 Draw a thin rectangle for the patty.

2 Draw the tomato and lettuce.

3 Make two half circles for the bun. Add a face and color.

Milkshake

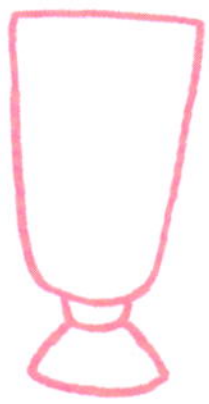

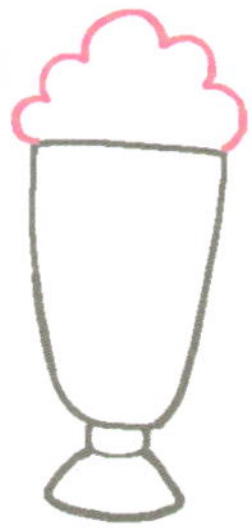

1 Draw a cup.

2 Add a fluffy cloud of whipped cream over the top of the cup.

3 Add a straw and a face.

MENU

Doodle your favorite foods onto this menu, or make up a sweet special of your own.

WHAT MAKES IT CUTE?

What makes a doodle adorable? It's all about the way stuff measures up, also known as *proportions*. Let's break it down on Ms. Panda here.

GET CUTER

Here's how to make your art even more adorable.

Make it round: Skip the corners and keep everything round and squishy.

Add tiny accessories: A teeny ice-cream cone or a tiny tiara could be the perfect finishing touch.

Mini-me: Draw a smaller version of your doodle to give it a mini-me.

Say anything: Give your critter something sweet to say in a voice bubble (page 56).

The Bear-y Bunch

Practice your proportions by tracing in the missing halves of these bears. Don't forget to add color!

KOALA BEAR

POLAR BEAR

GRIZZLY BEAR

SLOTH BEAR

BESPECTACLED BEAR

HIBERNATING BEAR

PURRR-FECT PET PALS

Kitty

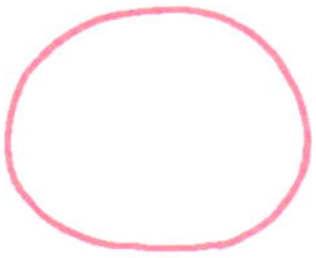

1 Draw an oval for the head.

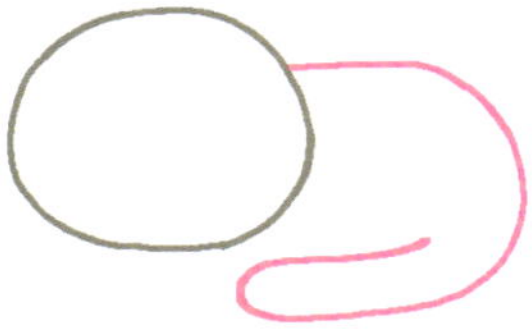

2 Draw a backward G for the body and tail.

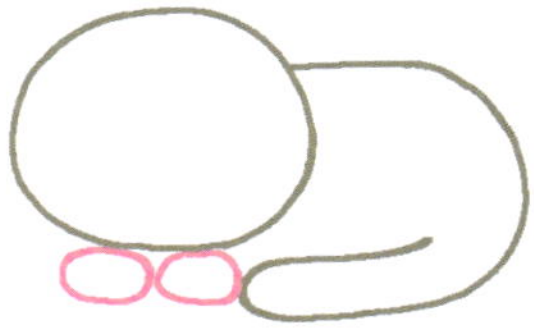

3 Add two small circles for paws.

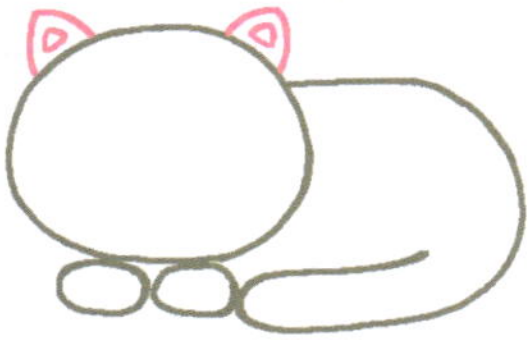

4 Sketch in triangles for ears.

5 Add stripes, whiskers, and a face.

6 Color in your cat!

TIP

Try drawing your pet pal in different positions. You don't always have to draw all the arms and legs.

Puppy

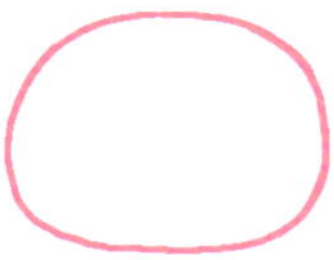

1 Draw an oval for the head.

2 Add a square for the body.

3 Draw in legs.

4 Add ears, a muzzle, and a tail.

5 Draw a face and a collar.

6 Color in your pup!

TEACUP CRITTERS

These mugs, rugs, and tiny baskets are just waiting
to be filled with precious pets.

BARNYARD BUDDIES

Goat

1 Draw an oval for the head. Add the body and legs.

2 Add ears, front legs, and a tail.

3 Draw the face. Don't forget the horns!

4 Color in your goat.

Piggy

1 Draw an oval for the head. Add a square body.

2 Add the arms and ears.

3 Draw a face. Add in a curly tail.

4 Color in your piggy.

Cow

1 Draw an oval for the head. Add a square body.

2 Add the arms and legs.

3 Draw the ears, horns, and a tail.

4 Add a face.

5 Sketch in a collar with a little bell.

6 Color in your cow and add spots.

TIP

Add patterns to your ani-pals (page 40).

KNOCK, KNOCK!

Which of your farm friends are at the door? Draw them in.

CUTIE COMBOS

What's a cutie combo? It's when you take two adorable things and mix them up into one doodle!

Pepperoni Pizza

+

Puppy

=

Pup-peroni Pizza

DRAW YOUR OWN

KITTY DONUT

Trace over the lines to start off this cutie combo. Then add a face, whiskers, and other details.

Kitty

+

Donut

=

MIX IT UP

Need more ideas for your cutie combos?
Try tracing the formula answers below.

Hamster

Ice-Cream Sundae

Hammy Sundae

Strawberry

Bunny

Bunny Berry

Cupcake

Hedgehog

Hedgie-Cake

WHERE MY PEEPS AT?

Girl

1 Draw a circle.

2 Sketch in the hair and neck.

3 Draw the body.

4 Add arms and draw a shirt collar.

5 Draw legs and feet.

6 Color in your peep!

MORE PEEPS

Here are more ideas for how to doodle more peeps.

Oh, boys:
To draw a boy, just change up the hair and clothes.

Dress to impress:
Experiment with different outfits and accessories (pages 28-29).

Strike a pose:
Add some bend to the arms and legs of your peeps to get them moving.

COMPLETE THE PEEP

Draw in outfits and hair to make these peeps perfect.

TIP

Remember to give your peeps a mood! Turn to page 12 for ideas.

ACCESSORIZE A to Z

Can't think of ideas to dress up your cute creations? Here's an alphabet of accessories for you to choose from. Doodle in your own ideas, too!

Apron

Buttons

Charm bracelet

Diadem (a kind of tiara)

DRAW SOMETHING THAT STARTS WITH C

Earmuffs

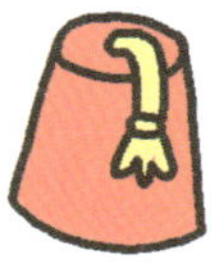

Fez

Glasses

Hat

Ice skates

Jacket

DRAW SOMETHING THAT STARTS WITH M

Kerchief

DRAW YOUR FAVE ACCESSORY!

Luggage

Mittens

Necklace

Obi sash

Peacoat

Quilted purse

Rain boots

DRAW SOMETHING
THAT STARTS WITH S

Sneakers

Tie

Umbrella

Vest

Watch

DRAW ANY
ACCESSORY
YOU WANT!

X-ray goggles

Yo-yo

Zipper

CUTIE COMBOS

It's easy to create cutie combos with peeps and animals—you can just draw a critter costume.

One Hoppy Kid

Frog

+

Boy

=

DRAW YOUR OWN

BEAR-Y CUTE PAL

Trace over the lines to start off this cutie combo. Then add a face and other details.

Bear

+

Girl

=

ADD IT UP

Trace the cutie combos below. Use the last row to make up your own peep and critter pairing.

Penguin

+

Girl

=

A Cool Chick

Red Panda

+

Girl

=

Panda Peep

YOUR TURN!

+ =

THE GREAT OUTDOORS

Bring Mother Nature in with these ideas for your art.

Draw different environments, like the beach or a snowy meadow.

Try drawing lots of different types of trees.

Flowers are always super sweet.

Mountains and hills add height to backgrounds.

Don't forget the weather! Is it a sunny day or dark and stormy?

PICTURE PERFECT

Fill these frames with sweet outdoorsy doodles.

WILD AT HEART

Elephant

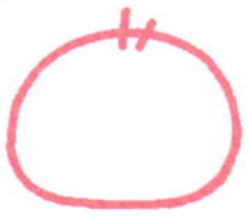

1 Sketch an oval for the head. Add two lines for hairs.

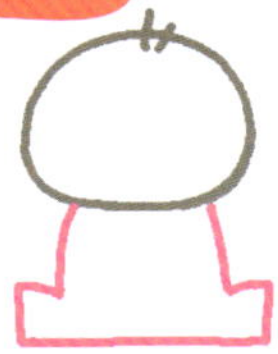

2 Draw a body with two legs.

3 Add four lines for front legs.

4 Draw two round ears.

5 Add a face and a trunk.

6 Add color and ink the outlines (remember to erase the pencil).

Monkey

1 Draw an oval for the head. Sketch a heart inside for the face.

2 Add two ears.

3 Draw a face and a little tuft of hair.

4 Sketch in a small body with a circle for the belly.

5 Add arms, legs, and a tail.

6 Add color and ink the outlines of your monkey.

ON SAFARI

Draw in some ani-pals for these jungle critters.

IN THE WOODS

Owl

1 Draw a round body. Make two small ear tufts on top.

2 Sketch in wings. Add scallops for feathers.

3 Draw a line across the body. Make small V's for feathers.

4 Add a face.

5 Draw two feet.

6 Add color, ink the outlines, and erase your pencil marks.

Raccoon

1 Draw a pointed oval for the head. Sketch a heart shape inside.

2 Add a face and ears.

3 Draw two circles around the eyes. Draw a body.

4 Sketch in tiny arms and legs.

5 Add a striped tail.

6 Add color to your art.

CAMP OUT

Fill in the rest of these merit badges with animals or anything else you want. Try to think of the skills that you'd earn your badges for, and write them in, too.

ON THE HIGH SEAS

Octopus

1 Draw a circle for the body.

2 Add skinny U's under the body for tentacles.

3 Sketch a face.

4 Add spots.

5 Give your octopus some bubbles.

6 Add color to your octopus.

Whale

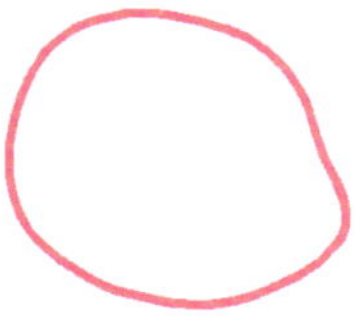

1 Draw a roundish shape.

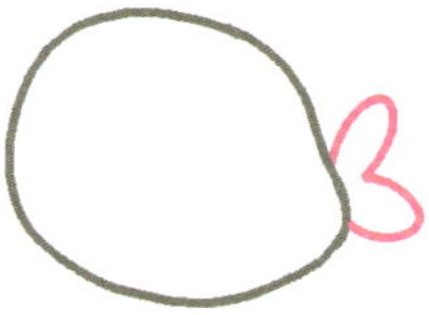

2 Add a tail to the end.

3 Give your whale a face.

4 Make small U's for fins.

5 Draw in the belly and add a spout.

6 Add color to your whale.

AYE, CAPTAIN!

You're the captain of your own submarine.
What can you see out of your sub's periscope?
Draw in your underwater seascape here.

1 Draw an oval, and add lines.

2 Add windows, a propeller, and a periscope.

3 Color in your submarine.

DOTS, DASHES & MORE

Got a lot of blank space in your sketchbook? Fill it up with super-duper easy patterns! Check out the ideas below.

TIP

Combine patterns together! Try making stripes inside your polka dots or scallops in your checkerboard pattern.

PRETTY KITTIES

Give these kitties their own style by adding some simple patterns.

MONSTER-IFIC

When it comes to monsters, there are no rules!
Anything you can doodle will make a mighty cute monster.

A monster can be pink and fluffy . . .

. . . or it can be blobby and squishy.

TIP

Try adding some patterns from page 40 for fun.

Long legs are great for monsters that do a lot of walking.

Add extra arms if your monster likes to hug.

Some monsters have lots of eyes (and eyelashes)!

Horns can help a monster snag some tasty snacks.

Don't forget to give your monster a mood (page 12)! Is your monster a happy critter, or is it feeling a bit grumpy?

MORE BEASTIES

Doodle in more details on the monsters below to make them your own.

MYTHS & MAGIC

TIP
Skip the horn of your unicorn and you've got a pony!

Unicorn

1 Draw the head.

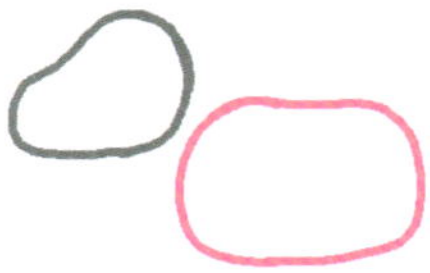

2 Add the body.

3 Sketch in the face. Add a neck between the head and body.

4 Draw in the legs. Add an ear.

5 Sketch in the horn, mane, and tail.

6 Add color, ink the outlines, and erase your pencil marks.

Yeti

1 Draw a hairy body.

2 Add arms and legs.

3 Draw two ovals for the face and belly.

4 Sketch a face.

5 Add two horns.

6 Color in your new yeti buddy.

CRAFT IT CUTE

You don't always have to use your markers to decorate your doodles. Check out this page for ways to add other craft supplies to your art.

Try coloring in your artwork with colored pencils, gel pens, or even watercolors.

Add stickers to your art to create sweet details.

Use a white gel pen to draw in details over a dark color.

Add some sparkle! Use glue to apply loose glitter to your doodles. Or glue on sequins or gems to add shine.

ADD COLOR!

AROUND TOWN

Your cute characters need fun places to hang out.
Color in the ideas below and draw your own tiny town.

A Sweet Street

Fill in this empty street with buildings and other stuff to make your very own village.

GADGETS & GIZMOS

Anything can be made cuter, even the stuff you use every day.
Get inspired by the ideas below and color them in.

INSIDE MY BACKPACK

Grab your bag and draw all the things you find inside it on the backpack below. Remember: Make it cute!

CUTIE COMBOS

Are you ready for more cutie combos? This time we're mashing up critters with gadgets and gizmos.

Piggy Alarm Clock

Pig

+

Clock

=

DRAW YOUR OWN

MONKEY PHONE

Trace over the lines to start off this cutie combo. Then add a face and other details.

Monkey

+

Phone

=

MAKE A MATCH

Pick a gizmo from the top of the page and combine it with a critter from the bottom to create an original cutie combo (like a cow-culator).

SHAPING UP

Got some empty spaces that need doodle love?
Try the simple shapes below to banish those blank spaces!

TIP

You can fill spaces with any small shape, like flowers (page 32).

UP IN OUTER SPACE

Fill up the empty spaces in this far-out drawing with stars, moons, and anything else you can think of. Then color them in.

WORDY WAYS

Got something to say? Say it with your doodles!
Here's how to add words to your art.

Word Burst

1 Draw "AWESOME!" in bubble letters.

2 Draw a voice bubble around it.

3 Add color and more doodles.

Pow Burst

1 Draw "POW"! Make it big and bold.

2 Add a pointy burst shape around it.

3 Add color and dimension lines if you want.

TRY YOUR OWN HERE!

LETTER IT

Here are more ideas for your word art.

fancy

LEANING

OFFICIAL

CLOUDS

OUTLINED

STRIPES

lowercase

BUBBLE

SKINNY

swooshy

TRY YOUR OWN HERE!

ADD YOUR OWN DOODLES TO THIS CUTIE KABLOOIE!

A CUTIE KABLOOIE

Turn your doodles into one big cluster, like the page on the left.
It's what we like to call a cutie kablooie, since it's an explosion of cuteness.

WHAT YOU'LL NEED:

- Tracing paper or thin sheet of paper
- Scissors
- Pencil
- Eraser
- Ink pen
- Markers

1. Take some of your favorite doodles from your sketchbook and trace them onto a piece of tracing paper.

2. Cut out the doodles one by one.

3. Arrange the cutouts any way you want. Place the bigger doodles first, then the smaller ones. Try taping them so they stay together.

4. Copy the arrangement onto a clean sheet of paper.

5. Fill up the empty spaces with patterns (page 40) or add words.

6. Color it in!

MORE CUTIE KABLOOIES

What should you put in your cutie kablooies?
Here are a few ideas to inspire your doodling.

Pretty Poses

Pick a character and draw it in different poses or doing different activities.

Groupies

Pick a category, like the ocean, and draw only things from that category.

Color Coordinate

Pick a color or a pattern to theme your kablooie.

My Favorite Things

Time to make your own cute clusters out of your faves!
We picked some themes below for you to draw.

Draw stuff that's your favorite color.

Draw your favorite snacks.

Draw your favorite ani-pals.

Draw your favorite books.

CREDITS

EDITOR:
F. S. Kim

ILLUSTRATORS:
Lauren Lowen & Lizzy Doyle

DESIGNER:
Lizzy Doyle

BUYER:
Sam Walker

MANAGING EDITOR:
Gina Kim

SPECIAL THANKS TO:
Stacy Lellos, Netta Rabin, Hannah Rogge, April Chorba, Kelly Shaffer, Barrie Zipkin, Owen Keating & Vanessa Han